Silver Dolphin Books
An imprint of Printers Row Publishing Group
A division of Readerlink Distribution Services, LLC
10350 Barnes Canyon Road, Suite 100, San Diego, CA 92121
www.silverdolphinbooks.com

All notations of errors or omissions should be addressed to Silver Dolphin Books,
Editorial Department, at the above address.
All other correspondence (author inquiries, permissions) concerning the content
of this book should be addressed to:
Elephant & Bird Books
201, Parkway House, Sheen Lane
London SW14 8LS. U.K.

ISBN: 978-1-68412-673-6
Manufactured, printed, and assembled in Heshan, China. LP/12/18.
22 21 20 19 18   1 2 3 4 5

Mother Goose's Classic Nursery Rhymes

Susie Brooks &
Sally Payne

Silver Dolphin

Contents

Old Mother Goose

Old Mother Goose,
When she wanted to wander,
Would ride through the air
On a very fine gander.

Mother Goose had a house,
It was built in a wood.
An owl at the door
As a porter stood.

She had a son Jack,
A plain-looking lad.
He was not very good,
Nor yet very bad.

She sent him to market,
A live goose he bought.
"Look, Mother!" he said,
"I did not go for naught."

Jack's goose and her gander
Soon grew very fond.
They'd both eat together,
Or swim in the pond.

Then Jack found one morning,
As I have been told,
His goose had laid him
An egg of pure gold.

Jack rode to his mother,
The news for to tell.
She called him a good boy
And said it was well.

Then Old Mother Goose,
She found the goose soon,
And mounting its back,
Flew up to the moon.

Little Bo-Peep

Little Bo-Peep has lost her sheep,
And can't tell where to find them.
Leave them alone, and they'll come home,
Wagging their tails behind them.

Little Bo-Peep fell fast asleep,
And dreamt she heard them bleating.
But when she awoke, she found it a joke,
For they were still a-fleeting.

Then up she took her little crook,
Determined for to find them.
She found them indeed, but it made her heart bleed,
For they'd left their tails behind them.

It happened one day, as Bo-Peep did stray
Into a meadow hard by.
There she espied their tails side by side,
All hung on a tree to dry.

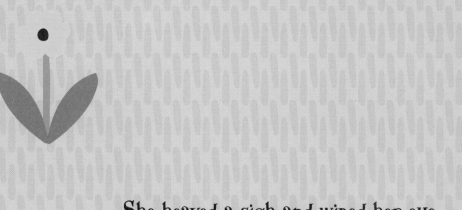

She heaved a sigh and wiped her eye,
And over the hillocks went rambling,
And tried what she could, as a shepherdess should,
To tack each again to its lambkin.

Hickory, Dickory, Dock

Hickory, dickory, dock,
The mouse ran up the clock.
The clock struck one,
The mouse ran down,
Hickory, dickory, dock.

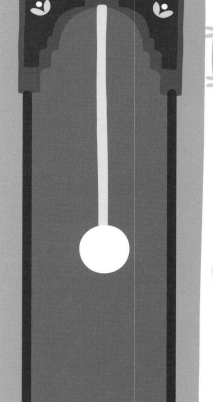

Dickory, Dickory, Dare

Dickory, dickory, dare,
The pig flew up in the air.
The man in brown
Soon brought him down,
Dickory, dickory, dare.

The House that Jack Built

This is the house that Jack built.

This is the malt
That lay in the house that Jack built.

This is the rat,
That ate the malt
That lay in the house that Jack built.

This is the cat,
That killed the rat,
That ate the malt
That lay in the house that Jack built.

This is the dog,
That worried the cat,
That killed the rat,
That ate the malt
That lay in the house that Jack built.

This is the cow with the crumpled horn,

That tossed the dog,

That worried the cat,

That killed the rat,

That ate the malt

That lay in the house that Jack built.

This is the maiden all forlorn,

That milked the cow with the crumpled horn,

That tossed the dog,

That worried the cat,

That killed the rat,

That ate the malt

That lay in the house that Jack built.

This is the man all tattered and torn,

That kissed the maiden all forlorn,

That milked the cow with the crumpled horn,

That tossed the dog,

That worried the cat,

That killed the rat,

That ate the malt

That lay in the house that Jack built.

This is the priest all shaven and shorn,

That married the man all tattered and torn,

That kissed the maiden all forlorn,

That milked the cow with the crumpled horn,

That tossed the dog,

That worried the cat,

That killed the rat,

That ate the malt

That lay in the house that Jack built.

This is the cock that crowed in the morn,

That woke the priest all shaven and shorn,

That married the man all tattered and torn,

That kissed the maiden all forlorn,

That milked the cow with the crumpled horn,

That tossed the dog,

That worried the cat,

That killed the rat,

That ate the malt

That lay in the house that Jack built.

This is the farmer sowing the corn,

That kept the cock that crowed in the morn.

That woke the priest all shaven and shorn,

That married the man all tattered and torn,

That kissed the maiden all forlorn,

That milked the cow with the crumpled horn,

That tossed the dog,

That worried the cat,

That killed the rat,

That ate the malt

That lay in the house that Jack built.

To Market

To market, to market, to buy a fat pig,
Home again, home again, jiggety jig.
To market, to market, to buy a fat hog,
Home again, home again, jiggety jog.
To market, to market, to buy a plum bun,
Home again, home again, market is done.

MARKET

20

Baa, Baa, Black Sheep

Baa, baa, black sheep,
Have you any wool?
Yes, sir, yes, sir,
Three bags full.
One for the master,
And one for the dame,
And one for the little boy
Who lives down the lane.

Three Blind Mice

Three blind mice,
Three blind mice,
See how they run!
See how they run!
They all ran after the farmer's wife,
Who cut off their tails with a carving knife.
Did you ever see such a thing in your life,
As three blind mice?

The Little Bird

Once I saw a little bird
Come hop, hop, hop,
So I cried, "Little bird,
Will you stop, stop, stop?"
And was going to the window
To say, "How do you do?"
But he shook his little tail,
And far away he flew.

The Clever Hen

I had a little hen, the prettiest ever seen,

She washed me the dishes and kept the house clean,

She went to the mill to fetch me some flour,

She brought it home in less than an hour,

She baked me my bread, she brewed me my ale,

She sat by the fire and told many a fine tale.

24

Little Robin Redbreast

Little Robin Redbreast sat upon a tree,

Up went Pussy-Cat, down went he,

Down came Pussy-Cat, away Robin ran,

Says little Robin Redbreast, "Catch me if you can!"

Little Robin Redbreast jumped upon a spade,

Pussy-Cat jumped after him, and but he was not afraid.

Little Robin chirped and sang, and what did Pussy say?

Pussy-Cat said: "Mew, mew, mew," and Robin flew away.

Mary Had a Little Lamb

Mary had a little lamb,
Its fleece was white as snow,
And everywhere that Mary went,
The lamb was sure to go.

It followed her to school one day,
Which was against the rule,
It made the children laugh and play,
To see a lamb at school.

And so the teacher turned it out,
But still it lingered near,
And waited patiently about
Till Mary did appear.

"What makes the lamb love Mary so?"
The eager children cried,
"Why, Mary loves the lamb, you know!"
The teacher did reply.

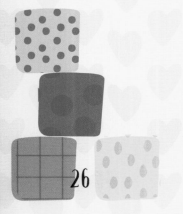

Puss Came Dancing

Puss came dancing out of a barn,
With a pair of bagpipes under her arm.
She could sing nothing but Fiddle-cum-fee,
The mouse has married the bumblebee.
Pipe, cat! Dance, mouse!
We'll have a wedding at our good house.

Horsie, Horsie

Horsie, horsie, don't you stop,
Just let your feet go clippety clop,
Your tail goes swish and the wheels go round,
Giddy up, we're homeward bound.

Steady Neddy, off you trot,
Just let your feet go clippety clop,
Your tail goes swish and the wheels go round,
Giddy up, we're off to town.

Horsie, horsie, don't you stop,
Just let your feet go clippety clop,
Your tail goes swish and the wheels go round,
Giddy up, we're homeward bound.

This Is the Way

This is the way the ladies ride,
Tri, tre, tre, tree,
Tri, tre, tre, tree!
This is the way the ladies ride,
Tri, tre, tre, tre, tri-tre-tre-tree!

This is the way the gentlemen ride,
Gallop-a-trot,
Gallop-a-trot!
This is the way the gentlemen ride,
Gallop-a-gallop-a-trot!

This is the way the farmers ride,
Hobbledy-hoy,
Hobbledy-hoy!
This is the way the farmers ride,
Hobbledy-hobbledy-hoy!

Cushy Cow

Cushy cow, bonny, let down your milk,

And I will give you a gown of silk,

A gown of silk and a silver tee,

If you will let down your milk to me.

Donkey, Donkey

Donkey, Donkey,
Old and gray,
Open your mouth
And gently bray.
Lift your ears
And blow your horn,
To wake up the world
This sleepy morn.

MILK

Tom, Tom, the Piper's Son

Tom, Tom, the piper's son,

Stole a pig, and away he run,

The pig was eat,

And Tom was beat,

And Tom ran crying down the street.

Dame Trot and Her Cat

Dame Trot and her cat
Led a peaceable life,
When they were not troubled
With other folks' strife.
When Dame had her dinner,
Pussy would wait,
And was sure to receive
A nice treat from her plate.

33

Little Jumping Joan

Here am I, little jumping Joan,
When nobody's with me
I'm always alone.

Jack Be Nimble

Jack be nimble,
Jack be quick,
Jack jump over
The candlestick.

Mary, Mary Quite Contrary

Mary, Mary quite contrary,
How does your garden grow?
With silver bells and cockle-shells,
And pretty maids all in a row.

Daffodils

Daffy-down-dilly has come to town,
In a yellow petticoat and a green gown.

Tweedle-Dum and Tweedle-Dee

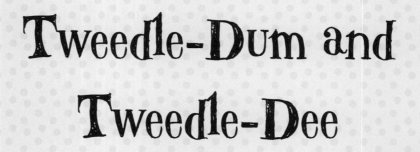

Tweedle-Dum and Tweedle-Dee
Resolved to have a battle,
For Tweedle-Dum said Tweedle-Dee
Had spoiled his nice new rattle.
Just then flew by a monstrous crow,
As big as a tar barrel,
Which frightened both the heroes so,
They quite forgot their quarrel.

Little Polly Flinders

Little Polly Flinders
Sat among the cinders,
Warming her pretty little toes.
Her mother came and caught her,
And scolded her young daughter,
For spoiling her nice new clothes.

There Was an Old Woman Who Lived in a Shoe

There was an old woman who lived in a shoe.

She had so many children she didn't know what to do.

She gave them some broth without any bread.

She hugged them and kissed them and put them to bed.

See-Saw, Margery Daw

See-saw, Margery Daw,
Jacky shall have a new master.
Jacky shall earn but a penny a day,
Because he can't work any faster.

Diddle Diddle Dumpling

Diddle diddle dumpling, my son John,
Went to bed with his breeches on,
One stocking off, and one stocking on,
Diddle diddle dumpling, my son John.

I'll Tell You a Story

I'll tell you a story
About Jack-a-Nory,
And now my story's begun.
I'll tell you another
About his brother,
And now my story is done.

There Was a Little Girl

There was a little girl,
And she had a little curl,
Right in the middle
Of her forehead.
When she was good,
She was very, very good,
But when she was bad,
She was horrid.

Curly-Locks

Curly-locks, Curly-locks, wilt thou be mine?
Thou shalt not wash the dishes, nor yet feed the swine,
But sit on a cushion and sew a fine seam,
And feed upon strawberries, sugar, and cream.

Dance to Your Daddie

Dance to your daddie,

My bonnie laddie,

Dance to your daddie, my bonnie lamb.

You shall get a fishy,

On a little dishy,

You shall get a fishy, when the boat comes home.

46

Dancy-Diddlety-Poppety-Pin

Dancy-diddlety-poppety-pin,
Have a new dress when summer comes in.
When summer goes out,
'Tis all worn out,
Dancy-diddlety-poppety-pin.

Jack and Jill

Jack and Jill went up the hill,

To fetch a pail of water.

Jack fell down and broke his crown,

And Jill came tumbling after.

Then up Jack got and home did trot,

As fast as he could caper,

He went to bed to mend his head,

With vinegar and brown paper.

Peter Piper

Peter Piper picked a peck of pickled peppers,
A peck of pickled peppers, Peter Piper picked.
If Peter Piper picked a peck of pickled peppers,
Where's the peck of pickled peppers Peter Piper picked?

Rain, Rain, Go Away

Come again another day.
Little Johnny wants to play,
Rain, rain, go away.

The Robin

The north wind doth blow,
And we shall have snow,
And what will poor robin do then,
Poor thing?
He'll sit in a barn,
And keep himself warm,
And hide his head under his wing,
Poor thing!

March Winds

March winds and April showers
Bring forth May flowers.

51

The Mulberry Bush

Here we go round the mulberry bush,
The mulberry bush, the mulberry bush,
Here we go round the mulberry bush,
On a cold and frosty morning.

This is the way we wash our hands,
Wash our hands, wash our hands,
This is the way we wash our hands,
On a cold and frosty morning.

This is the way we wash our clothes,
Wash our clothes, wash our clothes,
This is the way we wash our clothes,
On a cold and frosty morning.

This is the way we go to school,
Go to school, go to school,
This is the way we go to school,
On a cold and frosty morning.

This is the way we come out of school,
Come out of school, come out of school,
This is the way we come out of school,
On a cold and frosty morning.

Lucy Locket

Lucy Locket lost her pocket,
Kitty Fisher found it.
Nothing in it, nothing in it,
But the binding round it.

53

Little Girls

What are little girls made of, made of?
What are little girls made of?
Sugar and spice, and all things nice,
That's what little girls are made of!

54

Little Boys

What are little boys made of, made of?
What are little boys made of?
Frogs and snails, and puppy-dogs' tails,
That's what little boys are made of!

Ring-a-Ring o' Roses

Ring-a-ring o' roses,
A pocketful of posies,
A-tishoo! A-tishoo!
We all fall down.

Georgie Porgie

Georgie Porgie, pudding and pie,
Kissed the girls and made them cry.
When the boys came out to play,
Georgie Porgie ran away.

One for Sorrow

One for sorrow,
Two for joy,
Three for a girl,
Four for a boy,
Five for silver,
Six for gold,
Seven for a secret
Never to be told.
Eight for a wish,
Nine for a kiss,
Ten for a bird
You must not miss.

One, Two, Buckle My Shoe

One, two,
Buckle my shoe,
Three, four,
Knock at the door,
Five, six,
Pick up sticks,
Seven, eight,
Lay them straight,
Nine, ten,
A good fat hen,

Eleven, twelve,
Dig and delve,
Thirteen, fourteen,
Maids a-courting,
Fifteen, sixteen,
Maids in the kitchen,
Seventeen, eighteen,
Maids a-waiting,
Nineteen, twenty,
My plate's empty.

This Little Piggy

This little piggy went to market,

This little piggy stayed at home,

This little piggy had roast beef,

This little piggy had none,

And this little piggy cried, "Wee wee wee," all the way home.

One, Two, Three, Four, Five

One, two, three, four, five,

Once I caught a fish alive.

Six, seven, eight, nine, ten,

But I let it go again.

Why did you let it go?

Because it bit my finger so.

Which finger did it bite?

This little finger on the right.

As I Was Going to St. Ives

As I was going to St. Ives,
I met a man with seven wives,
Every wife had seven sacks,
Every sack had seven cats,
Every cat had seven kits.
Kits, cats, sacks, and wives,
How many were going to St. Ives?

A Counting-Out Rhyme

Hickery, dickery, six and seven,

Alabone, Crackabone, ten and eleven,

Spin, spun, muskidun,

Twiddle 'em, twaddle 'em, twenty-one.

1

2

3

65

Just Like Me

"I went up one pair of stairs."

"Just like me."

"I went up two pairs of stairs."

"Just like me."

"I went into a room."

"Just like me."

"I looked out of a window."

"Just like me."

"And there I saw a monkey."

"Just like me."

Cackle, Cackle, Mother Goose

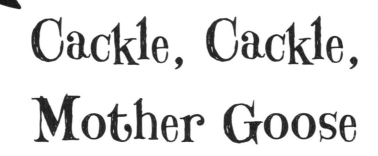

Cackle, cackle, Mother Goose,
Have you any feathers loose?
Truly have I, pretty fellow,
Half enough to fill a pillow.
Here are quills, take one or two,
And down to make a bed for you.

Chook, Chook, Chook-Chook-Chook

Chook-chook, chook-chook-chook,
Good morning, Mrs. Hen!
How many children do you have?
Madam, I have ten.
Four of them are yellow,
Four of them are brown,
And two of them are speckled red,
The nicest in the town.

Mrs. Mason's Basin

Mrs. Mason bought a basin.

Mrs. Tyson said, "What a nice 'un."

"What did it cost?" said Mrs. Frost.

"Half a crown," said Mrs. Brown.

"Did it indeed?" said Mrs. Reed.

"It did for certain," said Mrs. Burton.

Then Mrs. Nix, up to her tricks,

Threw the basin on the bricks.

The Man in the Wilderness

The man in the wilderness asked me
How many strawberries grew in the sea.
I answered him, as I thought good,
As many as red herrings grew in the wood.

Pop Goes the Weasel

Half a pound of tuppenny rice,
Half a pound of treacle.
That's the way the money goes,
Pop goes the weasel!

A penny for a spool of thread,
A penny for a needle,
That's the way the money goes,
Pop goes the weasel!

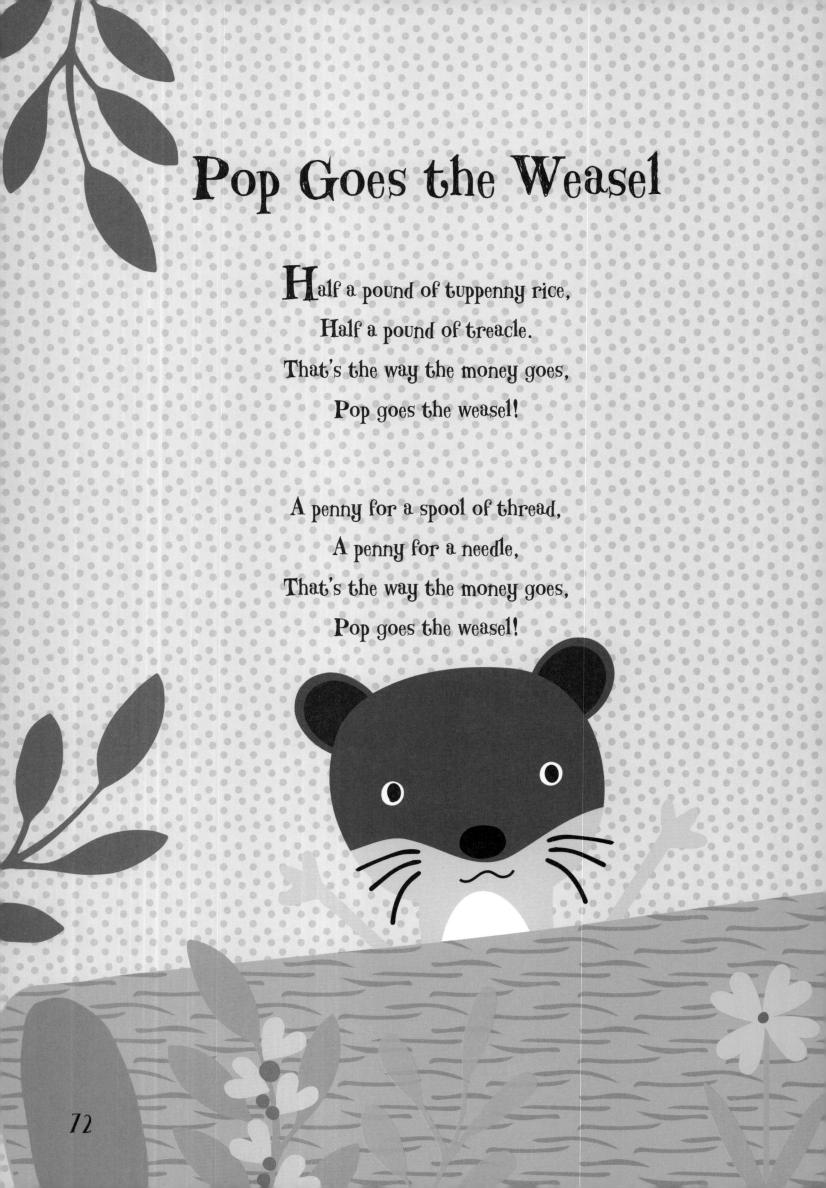

Half a pound of tuppenny rice,

Half a pound of treacle.

That's the way the money goes,

Pop goes the weasel!

Every night when I go out,

The monkey's on the table,

Take a stick and knock it off,

Pop goes the weasel!

Round and round the mulberry bush,

The monkey chased the weasel,

The monkey stopped to pull up his sock,

Pop goes the weasel!

Half a pound of tuppenny rice,

Half a pound of treacle,

Mix it up and make it nice,

Pop goes the weasel!

One, Two, Three, Four...

One, two, three, four,

Mary's at the cottage door,

Five, six, seven, eight,

Eating cherries off a plate.

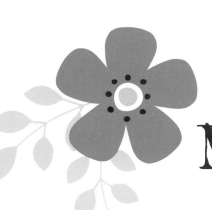

My Black Hen

Hickety pickety, my black hen,
She lays eggs for gentlemen.
Sometimes nine and sometimes ten,
Hickety pickety, my black hen.

Wibbleton Wobbleton

From Wibbleton to Wobbleton is fifteen miles,
From Wobbleton to Wibbleton is fifteen miles,
From Wibbleton to Wobbleton,
From Wobbleton to Wibbleton,
From Wibbleton to Wobbleton is fifteen miles.

To Babylon

How many miles to Babylon?
Three score and ten.
Can I get there by candlelight?
Yes, and back again!
If your feet are nimble and light,
You'll get there by candlelight.

Elizabeth

Elizabeth, Elspeth, Betsy, and Bess,
They all went together to seek a bird's nest.
They found a bird's nest with five eggs in,
They all took one, and left four in.

Play Days

How many days has my baby to play?
Saturday, Sunday, Monday,
Tuesday, Wednesday, Thursday, Friday,
Saturday, Sunday, Monday.

ABC

Great A, little a,
Bouncing B!
The cat's in the cupboard
And can't see me.

Calendar Days

Thirty days has September,

April, June, and November,

All the rest have thirty-one,

Excepting February alone,

Which has twenty-eight days clear,

And twenty-nine in each leap year.

Bees

A swarm of bees in May,

Is worth a load of hay.

A swarm of bees in June,

Is worth a silver spoon.

A swarm of bees in July,

Isn't worth a fly.

A Week of Birthdays

Monday's child is fair of face,

Tuesday's child is full of grace,

Wednesday's child is full of woe,

Thursday's child has far to go,

Friday's child is loving and giving,

Saturday's child works hard for a living,

But the child who is born on the Sabbath Day,

Is bonny and blithe and good and gay.

Sneezing

If you sneeze on Monday, you sneeze for danger,
Sneeze on a Tuesday, kiss a stranger,
Sneeze on a Wednesday, sneeze for a letter,
Sneeze on a Thursday, something better,
Sneeze on a Friday, sneeze for sorrow,
Sneeze on a Saturday, joy tomorrow.

Barber

Barber, barber, shave a pig,
How many hairs will make a wig?
Four and twenty, that's enough.
Give the barber a pinch of snuff.

Little Boy Blue

Little Boy Blue,

Come blow your horn!

The sheep's in the meadow,

The cow's in the corn.

But where is the boy, who looks after the sheep?

He's under a haystack, he's fast asleep.

Will you wake him? No, not I,

For if I do, he's sure to cry.

Humpty Dumpty

Humpty Dumpty sat on a wall,
Humpty Dumpty had a great fall.
All the King's horses and all the King's men
Couldn't put Humpty Dumpty together again.

For Want of a Nail

For want of a nail, the shoe was lost,

For want of the shoe, the horse was lost,

For want of the horse, the rider was lost,

For want of the rider, the battle was lost,

For want of the battle, the kingdom was lost,

And all for the want of a horseshoe nail.

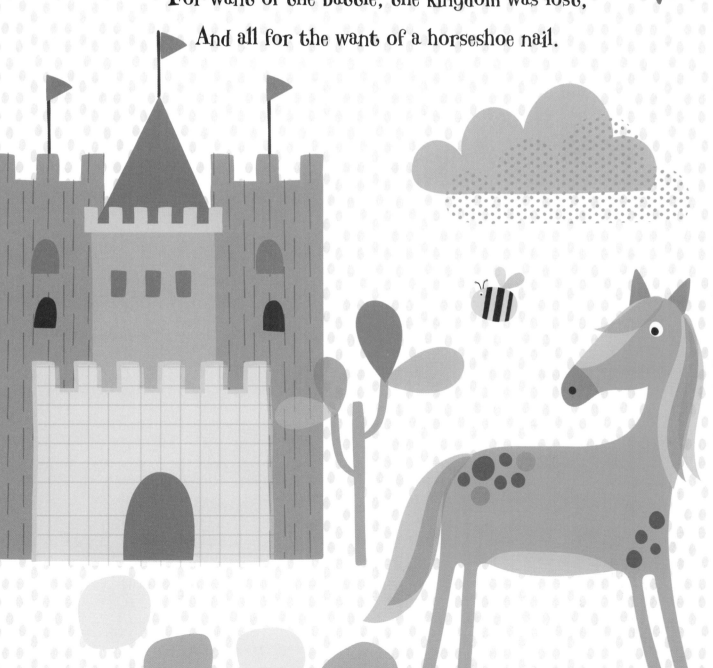

Sing a Song of Sixpence

Sing a song of sixpence,
A pocket full of rye,
Four-and-twenty blackbirds,
Baked in a pie.
When the pie was opened,
The birds began to sing,
Wasn't that a dainty dish
To set before the king?

The king was in his counting-house,
Counting out his money,
The queen was in the parlor,
Eating bread and honey.
The maid was in the garden,
Hanging out the clothes,
When down came a blackbird,
And pecked off her nose!

The Queen's Tarts

The Queen of Hearts,
She made some tarts,
All on a summer's day.
The Knave of Hearts,
He stole the tarts,
And took them clean away.
The King of Hearts
Called for the tarts,
And beat the Knave full sore.
The Knave of Hearts
Brought back the tarts,
And vowed he'd steal no more.

Pussy Cat, Pussy Cat

Pussy cat, pussy cat, where have you been?

I've been to London to visit the Queen.

Pussy cat, pussy cat, what did you there?

I frightened a little mouse, under her chair!

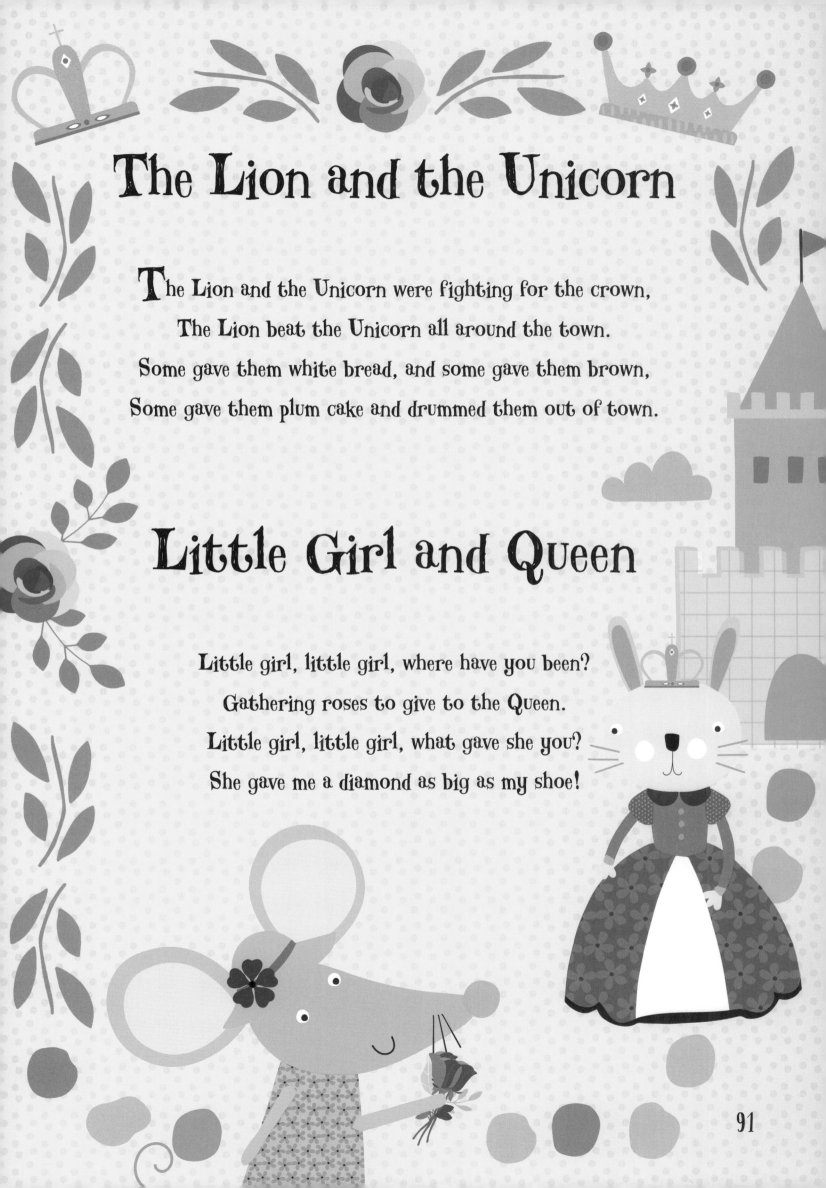

The Lion and the Unicorn

The Lion and the Unicorn were fighting for the crown,

The Lion beat the Unicorn all around the town.

Some gave them white bread, and some gave them brown,

Some gave them plum cake and drummed them out of town.

Little Girl and Queen

Little girl, little girl, where have you been?

Gathering roses to give to the Queen.

Little girl, little girl, what gave she you?

She gave me a diamond as big as my shoe!

Old King Cole

Old King Cole
Was a merry old soul,
And a merry old soul was he.
He called for his pipe,
And he called for his bowl,
And he called for his fiddlers three!
And every fiddler, he had a fine fiddle,
And a very fine fiddle had he.
Oh, there's none so rare
As can compare
With King Cole and his fiddlers three.

Doctor Foster

Doctor Foster went to Gloucester,

In a shower of rain.

He stepped in a puddle,

Right up to his middle,

And never went there again.

Banbury Cross

Ride a cock-horse to Banbury Cross,
To see a fine lady upon a white horse,
Rings on her fingers, and bells on her toes,
She shall have music wherever she goes.

BANBURY CROSS

Hector Protector

Hector Protector was dressed all in green,
Hector Protector was sent to the queen.
The queen did not like him,
No more did the king,
So Hector Protector was sent back again.

THE QUEEN

The Grand
Old Duke of York

Oh the grand old Duke of York,
He had ten thousand men,
He marched them up to the top of the hill,
And he marched them down again.

And when they were up, they were up,
And when they were down, they were down,
And when they were only halfway up,
They were neither up nor down.

I Saw a Ship a-Sailing

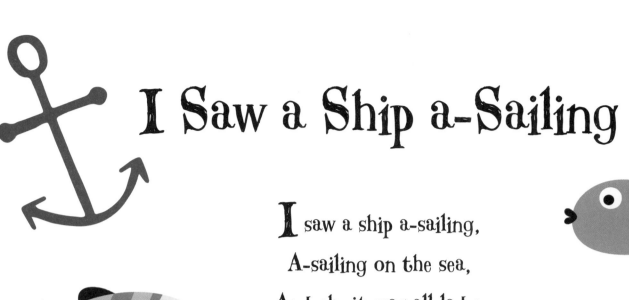

I saw a ship a-sailing,
A-sailing on the sea,
And oh, it was all laden
With pretty things for thee!
There were almonds in the cabin,
And apples in the hold,
The sails were made of silk,
And the masts were made of gold.

The four-and-twenty sailors
That stood between the decks,
Were four-and-twenty white mice,
With chains about their necks.
The captain was a duck,
With a packet on his back,
And when the ship began to move,
The captain said, "Quack! Quack!"

The Big Ship Sails

The big ship sails on the ally-ally-oh,
The ally-ally-oh, the ally-ally-oh,
Oh, the big ship sails on the ally-ally-oh,
On the last day of September.

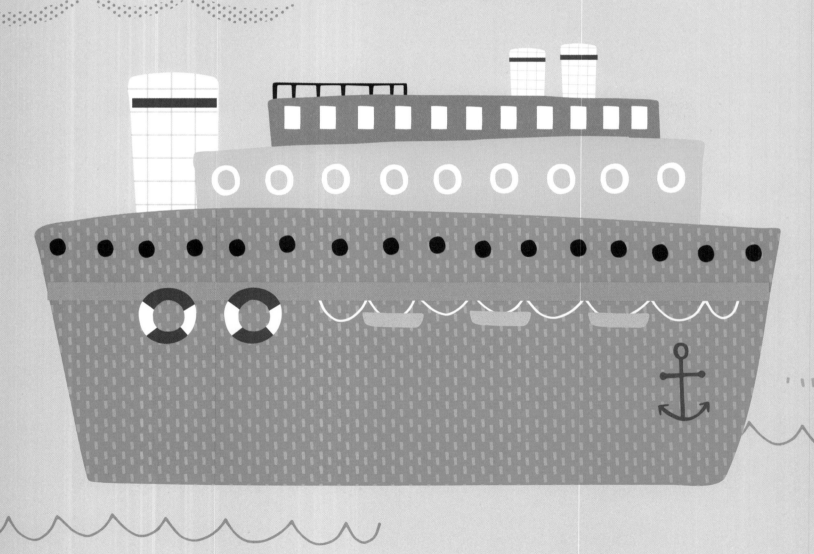

Three Wise Men of Gotham

Three wise men of Gotham
Went to sea in a bowl.
If the bowl had been stronger,
My song would be longer.

Cobbler, Cobbler

Cobbler, cobbler, mend my shoe,
Get it done by half-past two.
Half-past two is much too late!
Get it done by half-past eight.
Stitch it up and stitch it down,
And I will give you half a crown.

The Lost Shoe

Doodle doodle doo,
The Princess lost her shoe,
Her Highness hopped,
The fiddler stopped,
Not knowing what to do.

I Had a Little Nut Tree

I had a little nut tree,
Nothing would it bear,
But a silver nutmeg
And a golden pear.
The King of Spain's daughter
Came to visit me,
And all for the sake
Of my little nut tree.

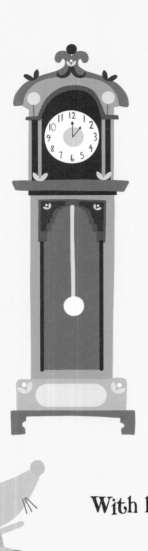

The Clock

There's a neat little clock,

In the schoolroom it stands,

And it points to the time

With its two little hands,

And may we, like the clock,

Keep a face clean and bright,

With hands ever ready to do what is right.

Down at the Station

Down at the station,
Early in the morning,
See the little puffer-billies,
All in a row.
See the engine driver
Pull his little lever,
Puff puff! Peep peep!
Off we go!

The Crooked Sixpence

There was a crooked man,

And he walked a crooked mile,

He found a crooked sixpence

Beside a crooked stile.

He bought a crooked cat,

Which caught a crooked mouse,

And they all lived together

In a little crooked house.

Lock and Key

"I am a gold lock."

"I am a gold key."

"I am a silver lock."

"I am a silver key."

"I am a brass lock."

"I am a brass key."

"I am a lead lock."

"I am a lead key."

"I am a don lock."

"I am a don key!"

London Bridge

London Bridge is falling down,
Falling down, falling down,
London Bridge is falling down,
My fair lady.

Build it up with wood and clay,
Wood and clay, wood and clay,
Build it up with wood and clay,
My fair lady.

Wood and clay will wash away,
Wash away, wash away,
Wood and clay will wash away,
My fair lady.

Build it up with bricks and mortar,
Bricks and mortar, bricks and mortar,
Build it up with bricks and mortar,
My fair lady.

Bricks and mortar will not stay,
Will not stay, will not stay,
Bricks and mortar will not stay,
My fair lady.

Build it up with silver and gold,
Silver and gold, silver and gold,
Build it up with silver and gold,
My fair lady.

Silver and gold will be stolen away,
Stolen away, stolen away,
Silver and gold will be stolen away,
My fair lady.

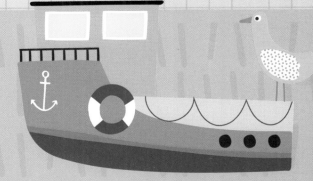

107

The Bells

"Oranges and lemons,"
Say the bells of St. Clement's.
"You owe me five farthings,"
Say the bells of St. Martin's.
"When will you pay me?"
Say the bells of Old Bailey.
"When I grow rich,"
Say the bells of Shoreditch.
"When will that be?"
Say the bells of Stepney.
"I do not know!"
Says the great bell of Bow.

Pairs or Pears

Twelve pairs hanging high,
Twelve knights riding by,
Each knight took a pear,
And yet left a dozen there.

Pat-a-Cake

Pat-a-cake, pat-a-cake, baker's man,

Bake me a cake, as fast as you can.

Roll it and pat it and mark it with a B,

And put it in the oven for baby and me.

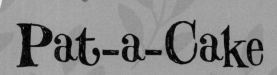

Baby Dolly

Hush baby, my dolly,

I pray you don't cry,

I'll give you some bread,

And some milk, by-and-by,

Or perhaps you like custard,

Or maybe a tart...

Then you're welcome to either,

With all of my heart.

Little Miss Muffet

Little Miss Muffet
Sat on a tuffet,
Eating her curds and whey.
Along came a spider,
And sat down beside her,
And frightened Miss Muffet away.

Little Jack Horner

Little Jack Horner
Sat in a corner,
Eating his Christmas pie.
He put in his thumb,
And pulled out a plum,
And said, "What a good boy am I!"

Old Mother Hubbard

Old Mother Hubbard
Went to the cupboard,
To give her poor dog a bone.
But when she got there,
The cupboard was bare,
And so the poor dog had none.

She went to the baker's
To buy him some bread,
When she came back,
The dog stood on his head!

She went to the hatter's
To buy him a hat.
When she came back,
He was feeding the cat.

She went to the barber's
To buy him a wig.
When she came back,
He was dancing a jig!

She went to the grocer's
To buy him some fruit.
When she came back,
He was playing the flute.

She went to the tailor's
To buy him a coat.
When she came back,
He was riding a goat!

She went to the cobbler's
To buy him some shoes.
When she came back,
He was reading the news.

She went to the seamstress
To buy him some linen.
When she came back,
The dog was a-spinning.

She went to the hosier's
To buy him some hose.
When she came back,
He was dressed in his clothes.

The dame made a curtsy,
The dog made a bow,
The dame said, "Your servant!"
The dog said, "Bow-wow."

Polly and Sukey

Polly put the kettle on,
Polly put the kettle on,
Polly put the kettle on,
We'll all have tea.

Sukey take it off again,
Sukey take it off again,
Sukey take it off again,
They've all gone away.

Coffee and Tea

Molly, my sister, and I fell out,
And what do you think it was all about?
She loved coffee and I loved tea,
And that was the reason we couldn't agree.

Jack Sprat

Jack Sprat could eat no fat,

His wife could eat no lean.

And so, between the two of them,

They licked the platter clean.

Peter, Peter, Pumpkin Eater

Peter, Peter, pumpkin eater,
Had a wife and couldn't keep her.
He put her in a pumpkin shell,
And there he kept her, very well.

Handy Pandy

Handy Pandy, Jack-a-dandy,
Loves plum cake and sugar candy.
He bought some at a grocer's shop,
And out he came, hop, hop, hop!

SHOP

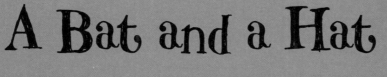

A Bat and a Hat

Bat, bat,

Come under my hat,

And I'll give you a slice of bacon.

And when I bake,

I'll give you a cake,

If I am not mistaken.

Simple Simon

Simple Simon met a pieman,
Going to the fair.
Said Simple Simon to the pieman,
"Let me taste your ware."
Said the pieman to Simple Simon,
"Show me first your penny,"
Said Simple Simon to the pieman,
"Sir, I haven't any."

Sing, Sing

Sing, sing, what shall I sing?

The cat's run away with the pudding string!

Do, do, what shall I do?

The cat's run away with the pudding too!

The Milkman

Milkman, milkman, where have you been?
In Buttermilk Channel, up to my chin.
I spilt my milk and I spoiled my clothes,
And I got a long icicle hung from my nose.

Blow Wind Blow

Blow wind blow,

And go mill go,

That the miller may grind his corn,

That the baker may take it

And into bread make it,

And bring us a loaf in the morn.

Pease Porridge

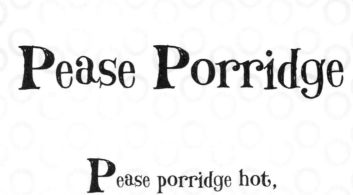

Pease porridge hot,
Pease porridge cold,
Pease porridge in the pot,
Nine days old.

Some like it hot,
Some like it cold,
Some like it in the pot,
Nine days old.

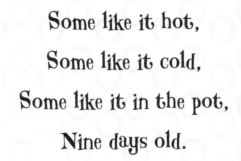

Hot Cross Buns

Hot cross buns!
Hot cross buns!
One a penny, two a penny,
Hot cross buns!
Give them to your daughters,
Give them to your sons,
One a penny, two a penny,
Hot cross buns!

129

Little Tommy Tucker

Little Tommy Tucker
Sings for his supper,
What shall he eat?
White bread and butter.
How will he cut it,
Without a knife?
How will he be married,
Without a wife?

130

Wash the Dishes

Wash the dishes,
Wipe the dishes,
Ring the bell for tea.
Three good wishes,
Three good kisses,
I will give to thee.

Little Fred

When little Fred went to bed,
He always said his prayers.
He kissed mama, and then papa,
And straightway went upstairs.

Bedtime

The Man in the Moon looked out of the moon,
Looked out of the moon and said,
"It's time for all children on the earth
To think about getting to bed!"

Dreams

Friday night's dream,
On Saturday told,
Is sure to come true,
Be it never so old.

Hey Diddle, Diddle

Hey diddle, diddle,

The cat and the fiddle,

The cow jumped over the moon.

The little dog laughed

To see such fun,

And the dish ran away with the spoon.

134

Early to Rise

Cocks crow in the morn
To tell us all to rise,
And those who sleep late
Will never be wise.
For early to bed,
And early to rise,
Is the way to be healthy
And wealthy and wise.

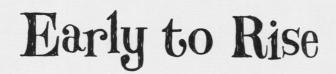

Girls and Boys

Girls and boys, come out to play,

The moon is shining, bright as day.

Leave your supper, and leave your sleep,

And join your playfellows in the street.

Come with a whoop, and come with a call,

Come with a good will or not at all.

Up the ladder and down the wall,

A tuppeny loaf will serve us all.

You bring milk and I'll bring flour,

And we'll have a pudding in half an hour.

137

The Man in the Moon

The Man in the Moon came down too soon,
And asked the way to Norwich.
He went by the south, and burnt his mouth
While eating cold pease porridge.

Old Woman, Old Woman

There was an old woman,

Tossed up in a basket,

Seventeen times as high as the moon.

Where was she going?

I just had to ask it,

For in her hand she carried a broom.

"Old woman, old woman, old woman," said I,

"Please tell me, why are you up so high?"

"I'm sweeping the cobwebs down from the sky,

And I'll be with you by-and-by!"

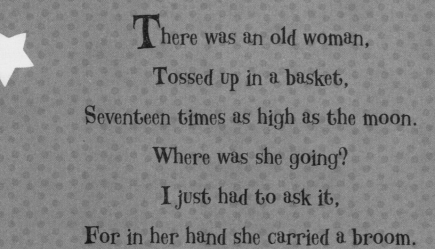

Rock-a-Bye

Rock-a-bye, baby, on the tree top,

When the wind blows the cradle will rock,

When the bough breaks the cradle will fall,

And down will come baby, cradle and all.

Sleep, Baby, Sleep

Sleep, baby, sleep,
Our cottage vale is deep,
The little lamb is on the green,
With woolly fleece so soft and clean.
Sleep, baby, sleep.

Sleep, baby, sleep,
Down where the woodbines creep,
Be always like the lamb so mild,
A kind and sweet and gentle child.
Sleep, baby, sleep.

Bye, Baby Bunting

Bye, baby bunting,

Daddy's gone a-hunting,

Mommy's gone a-milking,

Sister's gone a-silking,

And brother's gone to buy a skin

To wrap the baby bunting in.

Sleepyhead

"To bed! To bed!"
Says Sleepyhead,
"Let's wait a while,"
Says Slow.
"Put on the pan,"
Says hungry Nan,
"We'll eat before we go."

143

A Star

Higher than a house, higher than a tree.

Oh! Whatever can that be?

144

Prayers

Matthew, Mark, Luke, and John,

Bless the bed that I sleep on.

Four corners to my bed,

Four angels round my head,

Two to watch and two to pray

And keep me safe until the day.

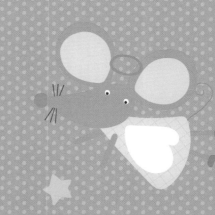

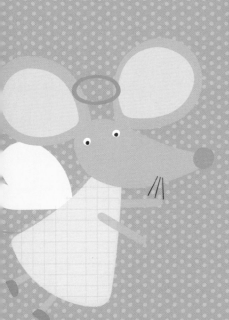

Wee Willie Winkie

Wee Willie Winkie runs through the town,

Upstairs and downstairs, in his nightgown,

Rapping at the window, crying through the lock,

"Are the children in their beds, for now it's eight o'clock?"

A Candle

Little Nanny Etticoat
In a white petticoat,
And a red nose.
The longer she stands,
The shorter she grows.

Hush Little Baby

Hush little baby, don't say a word,

Papa's going to buy you a mockingbird.

And if that mockingbird won't sing,

Papa's going to buy you a diamond ring.

And if that diamond ring turns to brass,

Papa's going to buy you a looking glass.

And if that looking glass gets broke,

Papa's going to buy you a billy goat.

And if that billy goat won't pull,

Papa's going to buy you a cart and bull.

And if that cart and bull turn over,

Papa's going to buy you a dog named Rover.

And if that dog named Rover won't bark,

Papa's going to buy you a horse and cart.

And if that horse and cart fall down,

You'll still be the sweetest little baby in town.

A Wish

Star light, star bright,
First star I see tonight.
I wish I may, I wish I might,
Have the wish I wish tonight.

I See the Moon

I see the moon, the moon sees me,
And the moon sees somebody I'd like to see.
God bless the moon and God bless me,
And God bless the somebody I'd like to see!

Sally Go Round the Sun

Sally go round the sun,
Sally go round the moon,
Sally go round the chimney tops,
Every afternoon.